A IS FOR AWESOME

DEDICATED TO

A IS FOR AWESOME

BY DALLAS CLAYTON

Candlewick Press

A IS FOR AWESOME AND ALSO AMAZIN'

B IS FOR **BEAUTIFUL**

BIG BOLD AND BRAZEN

C IS FOR CONFIDENT COOL AND COLLECTED

D IS FOR **DREAMING** THINGS NEVER EXPECTED

F IS FOR FOOLISH FANTASTICAL FUN

G IS FOR GREATNESS

YOU'RE WELL ON YOUR WAY

H IS FOR **HAPPY** TO SEE YOU TODAY

I is IMAGINE IDEAS ALL YOUR OWN

J JUST REMEMBER

YOU'RE NEVER ALONE

K IS FOR KIDS BEING KIDS (THAT'S THE COOLEST)

L IS FOR **LIVING LIFE** UP TO ITS FULLEST

M IS FOR THE MAKING MOST OF YOUR DAY

O is **OH BOY** THERE ARE SO MANY SIGHTS

P IS FOR **PASSION**

PURSUING WHAT'S RIGHT

Q IS FOR QUIET

TO ESCAPE FROM THE MADNESS

¿

R IS FOR

READING

BUT ALSO FOR RADNESS

S IS FOR

SAILING

IN ALL SEVEN SEAS

T IS FOR

TALKING

AND TEACHING
AND TREES

U

UNDERSTANDING

AND
THE
UNIVERSE

TOO

V IS FOR **VALUES**

AND KEEPING THEM TRUE

W FOR

WISDOM

BOTH SPOKEN
AND WRITTEN

X MARKS THE SPOT
WHERE THE

TREASURE
IS HIDDEN

Y IS FOR YOU.
THE BEST KID AROUND

MY NAME IS DALLAS CLAYTON.
I WROTE THIS BOOK AND DREW ALL THE PICTURES.
I HOPE YOU LIKE IT
AND I HOPE IT HELPS YOU LEARN
SOME NEW LETTERS
THAT YOU CAN USE
TO MAKE MAGICAL WORDS
AND SHARE BIG IDEAS!

First edition 2014

Library of Congress Catalog Card Number 2013934304
ISBN 978-0-7636-5745-1

13 14 15 16 17 18 CCP 10 9 8 7 6 5 4 3 2 1

Printed in Shenzhen, Guangdong, China

This book was hand-lettered by the author.
The illustrations were done in ink and watercolor.

Candlewick Press
99 Dover Street
Somerville, Massachusetts 02144

visit us at www.candlewick.com